Live Music!

Woodwinds

Elizabeth Sharma

Thomson Learning
New York

Books in the series

Brass   Strings
Keyboards   The Voice
Percussion   Woodwinds

First published in the
United States in 1993 by
Thomson Learning
115 Fifth Avenue
New York, NY 10003

First published in 1992 by
Wayland (Publishers) Ltd

Cataloging-in-Publication Data applied for

ISBN: 1-56847-115-7

Printed in Belgium by Casterman, s.a.,
Bound in Italy by L.E.G.O.

Contents

Woodwind instruments used to be made from wood, and air – wind – had to be blown through them to make the sound. It is obvious why they were called woodwinds. But today, many woodwind instruments are made out of plastic and metal.

Woodwind instruments are found all over the world. Some, like the Indian snake charmer's been, are played with a **reed**. Others, such as the recorder, just have a **mouthpiece**. Some are blown from the end and others – like the flute – from the side.

You will find several different kinds of woodwind instruments in a modern orchestra. In the front row you can see the flutes on the left, the oboes in the middle, and the clarinets on the right.

All that jazz

Here is a saxophone player. Jazz saxophone players invent their own long solos, called improvisations.

If you listen to some jazz music, you will hear the loud, bright sounds of the saxophones. Saxophones play exciting solos. The notes ripple up and down, from high shrieks to deep, low sounds.

There are four main sizes of saxophones: the soprano (the smallest), alto, tenor, and baritone (the largest). The most popular are the alto and tenor. The tenor sax has a big, loud sound.

Woodwind and brass instruments are loud enough to be heard out of doors, and they can be played while marching. You can see them in military bands and marching bands.

Here is a marching band of Scottish bagpipers. In Scotland the bagpipes are often played on special occasions.

Woodwinds of the orchestra

In the orchestra on the opposite page, the flutes play the highest notes. Sometimes an even higher woodwind, a baby flute called a piccolo, is played. The piccolo is the smallest instrument in the orchestra. Its high, shrill sound can be clearly heard even when the whole orchestra is playing.

Bassoon

Flute

Oboe

Clarinet

The oboe players sit near the flutists (flute players). The oboe has a reedy, **nasal** sound. One or two players may sometimes use the cor anglais. This has a lower **pitch** and softer sound than the oboe.

Then there are the clarinets. Sometimes you will hear a **bass** clarinet. *The Dance of the Sugar Plum Fairy* from *The Nutcracker Suite* by the Russian composer Peter Illich Tchaikovsky is the most famous bass clarinet solo.

The bassoons are the bass instruments of the woodwinds. The bassoon has been called "the clown of the orchestra" because it looks odd and can make funny, gruff sounds. But it also has a beautiful, rich, and expressive tone.

Blowing in the wind

Have you ever wondered why a musical sound comes out when you blow a recorder?

The body of the recorder is a tube. When you blow into the tube, the air inside it **vibrates**. This makes the sound.

A soprano recorder is a small tube. When you blow into it, you hear a high sound. A big, tenor recorder makes a low sound. The longer and wider the tube, the lower the sound produced.

The girl on the right is playing a tenor recorder, and the girl on the left is playing a soprano.

When you blow the recorder without covering the holes, it makes a high note. The air goes down the tube only a little way before it escapes through the holes.

If you cover all the holes with your fingers, and blow very, very gently into the recorder, you will notice that the note is much lower. That is

This girl is playing a high note on the soprano recorder.

because when the holes are covered the air has to travel all the way down to the end of the tube before it can escape.

Flute sounds

If you blow gently across the top of an empty bottle, you can produce a whistling sound. The air strikes the opposite side of the hole and sets the column of air in the bottle vibrating. This is how a flute works.

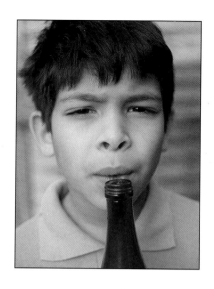

This boy is whistling across the top of a bottle.

There are many side-blown flutes all over the world, often made out of hollow bamboo. Listen to the sweet, expressive sound of Indian bamboo flute music, played by Hari Prasad Chaurasia of India.

Orchestral flutes developed from these simple instruments. In the 19th century, the German instrument-maker Theobald Boehm

This girl is playing an orchestral flute. The flute has a lip rest to make blowing across the hole more comfortable.

invented a clever system of keys for the flute, to make it easier to play and to make it sound better. Orchestral flutes were made of metal, not wood, so that the sound would carry better in a big orchestra.

The recorder has a shaped mouthpiece, and it is blown from the end, not the side. It is easier to blow than a flute. Try for yourself.

Simple recorders and flutes are used all over the world in folk music. They are cheap to make and light to carry around. Children can learn to play them quite easily. Some folk flutes are called penny whistles.

*This woman is playing a penny whistle. To play the notes an **octave** higher, she just has to blow harder.*

Single reds

Bend your thumbs around a blade of grass so that you are holding it with the top and base of your thumbs. Clasp your hands over the top and blow through the grass.

Have you ever held a leaf or a blade of grass between your thumbs and blown it to produce a squeak? The leaf vibrates and makes the sound. This is how the bamboo reed on a clarinet works. One end of it is attached to the clarinet mouthpiece.

Saxophones have the same kind of mouthpiece and reed as a clarinet. That is why they are counted as woodwind instruments, although the body of the instrument is made of brass. Clarinet and saxophone players learn to control the reed with their lips to produce a smooth sound with no squeaks.

Single Reeds

Clarinet · Bass Saxophone

This Indian snake charmer is playing a been. There is a single reed inside the instrument. The player's lips do not touch the reed, so he cannot control it. He must blow air smoothly to avoid squeaks.

Snake charming music is based on a musical phrase – a group of notes that go together to form part of a tune. The phrase is repeated often, just as the snake repeats the same movements to move along the ground.

Double reeds

Blow up a balloon, then stretch the neck sideways. You will hear a loud, squeaking sound as the air escapes. The neck of the balloon behaves rather like the double reed on oboes and bassoons. The air vibrates between the two sides of the neck.

This boy is stretching the neck of a balloon to make it squeak.

A double reed is made from a piece of cane folded over and slit across the top.

To make the oboe or bassoon sound, the player forces air between the two sides of the bamboo reed. This makes the column of air inside the instrument vibrate. The bassoon and oboe are very hard to play.

Bassoon reed

Bags of wind

One of the hardest things about playing a wind instrument is figuring out when to take a breath. Bagpipe players have solved this problem.

The piper blows into the bag to fill it with air. He or she squeezes the bag with one arm, and the air is pushed through a reed. The reed vibrates to make the sound. The player does not need to huff and puff! Bagpipes are found all over Europe, Africa, and Asia.

This young Scottish boy is being helped to play the bagpipes. The bagpipes make a loud, shrill sound called a skirl.

Woodwind instruments date back to prehistoric times. People found they could make a musical note by blowing across a hollow bone or the opening of a shell. In very early times, these sounds were probably used to make signals, rather than music for enjoyment.

These Quechua Indians from Peru are blowing into large conch shells.

The Chinese scale

It is said that a man called Ling Lun, chief musician to the Emperor of China, invented the Chinese **scale** in about 3000 B.C.

16

Ling Lun went to a valley of bamboo trees and cut tall, hollow poles of equal thickness. He used these to make a set of **pitch pipes**, called lü, to fix the notes of the Chinese scale.

Ling Lun worked out the length of each bamboo pipe compared to the longest and lowest one, using arithmetic. Blowing across the top of each pipe, he made a different note. See page 25 to find out how to make your own set of lü.

This Chinese man is playing a folk instrument called a sheng. It is made from bamboo pipes of different lengths, like Ling Lun's lü, but it is played differently. The player blows into the instrument, and the air goes up into the pipes.

Top notch

Woodwind instruments around the world developed from the early pipes. People noticed that the sound could be produced more easily if a **notch** was cut in the end of the tube, and the mouthpiece was shaped. Holes were cut in the pipe, which could be covered or uncovered by the fingers. So one pipe could produce many notes.

Woodwinds in Europe

In the 16th century, music was a very important part of the social life of educated people in Europe. Recorders were popular then, as now.

This Japanese man is playing a bamboo flute called a shakuhachi. It has a notch cut in the top.

In this late 17th or early 18th-century painting you can see two musicians holding simple flutes. These flutes were similar to recorders, but they were blown from the side.

They were used in orchestras until the 17th century. At that time the woodwind instruments of the modern orchestra were developed.

The oboe developed from the shawm, a Middle Eastern folk instrument with a double reed. The shawm reached Europe in medieval times. The word oboe comes from the French *haut bois*. This means "high wood."

Larger, lower-pitched kinds of oboes, with even more wonderful names, appeared in the orchestras of the 17th century. There was the *oboe d'amore* and the *oboe de caccia* (meaning the love oboe and the hunting oboe, in Italian). The bassoon also developed from the shawm, in about 1700.

This is an early 18th-century shawm. Orchestral oboes were made in the same long, narrow shape as the shawm.

The clarinet comes from Germany. It developed from a simpler instrument, called the chalumeau, in the late 17th century. The lower notes of the clarinet are still called the chalumeau register.

Wolfgang Amadeus Mozart wrote the first important concert music for the clarinet. Find a recording of his clarinet **concerto** and enjoy the sweet sounds of the instrument. Notice the mood of the music and how it changes.

Here is a modern picture of clarinet players.

The wind is blown around the world

Beautiful flutes can be found all over the world, made from bamboo, carved wood, or sometimes bone. Mostly, they have a simple set of holes. To play a note one octave higher, you just have to blow harder.

These Bolivian men are playing large wooden flutes.

Listen to some panpipe music from the Andes mountains of South America. Haunting sounds come from the pipes.

Each set of panpipes is really a collection of one-note flutes, like Ling Lun's lü. They are tied together in bundles so that the player can move quickly from one pipe to another. Panpipes come in all different sizes and pitches.

Ocarinas are egg-shaped flutes, usually with a mouthpiece and several finger holes.

This Mexican ocarina (above) is blown through a blowhole at the back, and it has one finger hole.

This man is playing the panpipes and the guitar at the same time.

Simple oboes and clarinets

Woodwind instruments are good for outdoor events like processions, since they can be played loudly. The man between the drummers in the picture above is playing the Indian oboe, the shehnai.

This is an alghaita, a kind of shawm from northern Nigeria. Players of the alghaita use a special way of breathing in through the nose and blowing out into the instrument through the mouth at the same time. They do not need to stop the flow of music to breathe. It is called circular breathing.

Some oboe players can do circular breathing. It is very difficult. Try it for yourself while playing a recorder.

This man is playing a shawm from Chad, northern Africa.

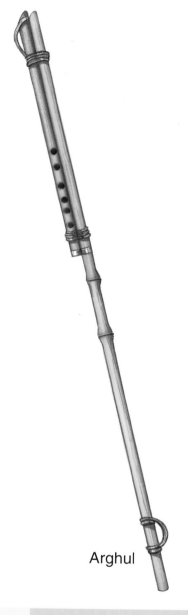

Simple versions of the clarinet are found all over the world. The arghul is a double clarinet from Egypt, with two joined tubes and two mouthpieces. The melody is usually played on the short tube. The long tube plays a **drone** to accompany the melody.

Arghul

Making pitch pipes

You can make a set of pitch pipes like Ling Lun's using plastic plumber's pipe instead of bamboo. You will need a metric ruler and about 2.5 meters of pipe, ¾ inch in diameter. Do the measuring yourself, but ask an adult to cut the pipe for you.

These boys are measuring and marking the plumber's pipe for their teacher to cut. Measurements must be exact.

1. Measure a length of 54 cm. This will be your lowest note, called the **fundamental**. Call this C, although it will not be exactly in tune with C on the piano.

2. A pipe two-thirds of the length of the fundamental will give the note G, a fifth higher. Two-thirds of 54 cm = 36 cm.

3. A pipe two-thirds of the length of the G pipe would give D, a fifth higher. That would be D above upper C. You should double the length to produce the D an octave lower. Two-thirds of 36 cm = 24 cm. Double it to make 48 cm.

4. A pipe two-thirds of the length of the D pipe would make A, a fifth higher. Two-thirds of 48 cm = 32 cm.

5. Two-thirds of the A pipe would produce upper E, a fifth higher, but as that would be outside the octave, double the length to give the E an octave lower. Two-thirds of 32 cm = 21.3 cm. Double it to make 42.6 cm.

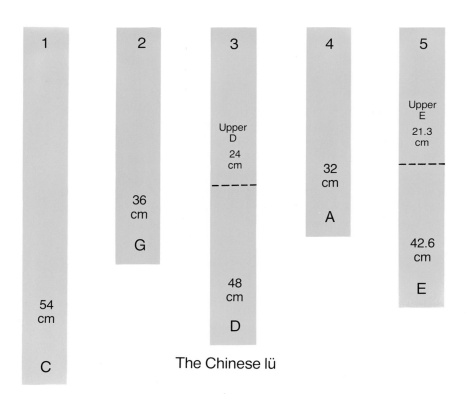

The Chinese lü

Playing your pitch pipes

The Chinese consider the first five pitch pipes, the lü, to be the most **harmonious**. These five notes, C, D, E, G, and A, make up the **pentatonic scale**. Much Chinese music is based on this scale.

Musicians in many other countries also like the pentatonic scale. It is used all over the world, particularly in folk music.

Five people can each hold one of the lü and blow gently across the top.

Each girl is playing one note of the pentatonic scale on pitch pipes made of plumber's pipe.

Blow again, this time with the palm of one hand blocking the bottom of the pipe. How many notes can you make from the five tubes now?

Try to play *Auld Lang Syne* with your lü. The line under some of the letters shows where the player must block the end of the tube.

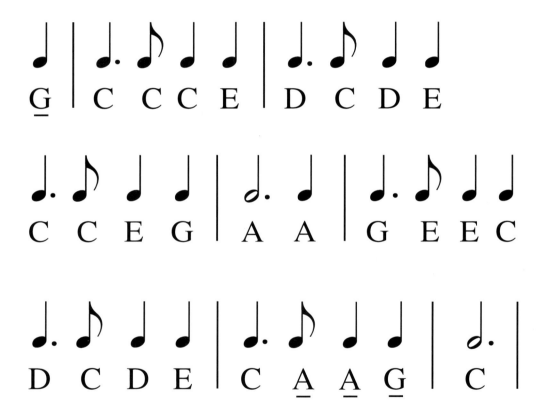

You could use a xylophone to compose another pentatonic **melody**. Write it out as shown above.

Here are a Russian and a Japanese
melody for you to play on recorders:

Little Bird – Russian melody

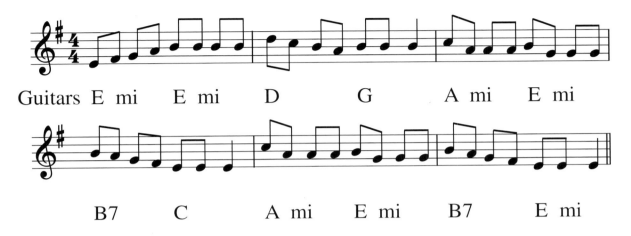

Guitars E mi   E mi   D   G   A mi   E mi

B7   C   A mi   E mi   B7   E mi

Sakura (Cherry Tree) – Japanese melody

This melody is composed in a
Japanese scale, and would be
played on a shakuhachi in Japan
(see page 18). It does not need a
piano or guitar **accompaniment**, but
you could add chime bars or some
suitable percussion instruments.

Glossary

Accompaniment The part played by an instrument, a voice, or an orchestra that accompanies the melody.

Bass The lowest and largest instrument in a family of musical instruments.

Concerto A piece of music written for a solo instrument accompanied by an orchestra.

Drone A bass note or chord played over and over again to accompany a melody.

Fundamental The lowest note that can be produced by a wind instrument.

Harmonious Tuneful and pleasing to the ear.

Melody The correct musical term for a tune.

Mouthpiece The part of a woodwind instrument into which the player blows.

Nasal Seeming as if the sound comes from the nose.

Notch A V-shaped cut.

Octave The eight-note distance between two musical notes of the same name but different pitch.

Pentatonic scale A scale that is made up of five notes. (Penta—comes from the Greek *pente*, and means five.) The most common pentatonic scale consists of C, D, E, G, and A.

Pitch How high or low a note is.

Pitch pipes A set of pipes that sound standard notes.

Reed A thin piece of cane or metal set in the mouthpiece of some wind instruments. It makes the air in the instrument vibrate when the player blows through it.

Scale A group of musical notes going up or down at fixed intervals.

Vibrates Shakes rapidly.

Finding out more

1. Why not listen to some woodwind music? Here are some ideas:

Clarinet and saxophone music: *Big Band Swing* by the Glenn Miller Band

Flute music: *James Galway plays Showpieces for Flute* by James Galway

Orchestral music: *The Young Person's Guide to the Orchestra* by Benjamin Britten

Rhapsody in Blue by George Gershwin. This orchestral music is in jazz and blues style. The clarinet is the solo woodwind instrument.

Shehnai music: *Fifty Golden Years of Bismillah Khan* by Bismillah Khan

2. Watch concerts on television. There are often programs of music from around the world.

3. Try to hear some live music. Keep an eye out for military bands playing in parks, youth marching bands, and pipe and drum bands. You can find out about these from your local library.

Useful books

Berger, Melvin. *The Science of Music*. New York: HarperCollins, 1989.

Greene, Carol. *Music*. Chicago: Childrens Press, 1983.

Mundy, Simon. *The Usborne Story of Music*. Tulsa: EDC, 1980.

Pillar, Marjorie. *Join the Band!*. New York: HarperCollins, 1992.

Wiseman, Ann. *Making Musical Things*. New York: Macmillan, 1979.

Index

Page numbers in **bold** indicate subjects shown in pictures as well as in the text.

Acknowledgments
The photographs in this book were provided by: C.M. Anderson 10 (below); Antonia Reeve Photography 19; Chapel Studios 7, 9, 10 (above), 14, 21, 22 (below); Compix (M. Proctor) 23 (above); East Sussex County Music Centre 20; E.T. Archive 18 (below); Eye Ubiquitous (G. Nikiteas) 4; Horniman Museum 23 (below); Hutchison 24; Japanese Information Centre 18 (above); Photri 13; Pitt Rivers Museum 22 (above); South American Pictures (T. Morrison) 16 and 21; Still Moving Picture Library 6,11 (P. Tomkins) 15; Wayland Picture Library (all Garry Fry) *cover*, 8, 12, 25, 27; ZEFA (W. Mueller) 5, (Xinhua-News) 17.
Artwork: Creative Hands 12, 14, 24, 26; Malcolm Walker 7.